Clap Your Hands

Lorinda Bryan Cauley

G. P. Putnam's Sons New York

G. P. Putnam's Sons,
a division of The Putnam & Grosset Book Group,
200 Madison Avenue, New York, NY 10016.
Published simultaneously in Canada
Printed in Hong Kong by South China Printing Co. (1988) Ltd.
Designed by Jean Weiss

Library of Congress Cataloging-in-Publication Data
Cauley, Lorinda Bryan.
Clap your hands / by Lorinda Bryan Cauley.   p.   cm.
Summary: Rhyming text instructs the listener to
find something yellow, roar like a lion,
give a kiss, tell a secret, spin in a circle,
and perform other playful activities.
[1. Play—Fiction. 2. Stories in rhyme.] I. Title.
PZ8.3.C3133C1   1992   91-12863 CIP AC   [E]—dc20
ISBN 0-399-22118-2
5   7   9   10   8   6   4

To my little girls, Sean and Erin

Clap your hands,
stomp your feet.

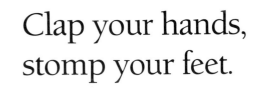

Shake your arms,
then take a seat.

Rub your tummy,
pat your head.

Find something yellow,
find something red.

Reach for the sky,
wiggle your toes.

Stick out your tongue
and touch your nose.

Wiggle your fingers,
slap your knee.

I'll tickle you
if you tickle me!

Find something big,
find something small.

Spin in a circle...
but try not to fall!

Close your eyes
and count to four.

Now do a somersault
across the floor.

Spread your feet,
look upside down.

Make a silly face
and act like a clown.

Hop like a bunny,
flap like a bird.

Quiet as a mouse, now…
Don't say a word!

Tell me your name.
How old are you?

Tell me a secret,
and I'll tell you one, too!

Purr like a kitten,
bark like a dog.

Crawl like a baby,
jump like a frog.

Fly like an airplane
high in the sky.

It's time to go now,
so wave bye-bye...

Bye-bye!